José's Christmas Secret

José's Christmas Secret

by Joan M. Lexau

Illustrated by Don Bolognese

THE DIAL PRESS   NEW YORK

pro Matička s láska

José's Christmas Secret

He was ten years old, and the man of the family. José shivered, but not from the cold.

"José, you are restless. Are you warm enough?" his mother whispered in Spanish. She usually spoke in English, but it did not seem natural to use a strange tongue in the dark.

"No, Mami," José answered in the same language. "It is not I who am cold. Why can you not take one of our warm blankets? Why do we need two? Tomás and I have each other to keep us warm." His seven-year-old brother slept with him on the mattress on the floor.

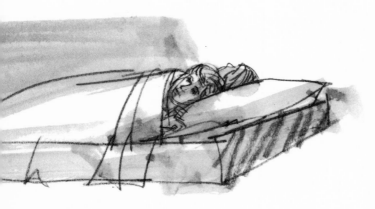

Every night he begged her to take one of the wool blankets, for hers were only cotton, and every night she said the same as now: "No, José. No, but thank you. You sleep near the floor where the cold air goes. I will be all right. Do not worry so, *mi hombrecito*."

She had started calling him that, "my little man," after his father died and he became the man of the house. But how could he help but worry? Ever since his father died of pneumonia last spring, his mother had looked frightened and alone.

José remembered, with a sick feeling in his stomach, how after the funeral she had wept and moaned at being stranded in a strange country. There was little money to go on with and no money to take them home to the island they had left only a month before. The money they had won in the lottery which had brought them to the mainland was almost gone, although they had thought it would last so long. If his father had died in Puerto Rico, relatives and neighbors would have come rushing to share with them what little they had. But here in New York even the neighbors were strangers.

The cold in this land seemed to creep into the minds of the people and chill their hearts. His mother said once, "It is not the same as it is on the island where you have so little it does not matter if you share it. You come here to do better and you work so hard for it, you do not want anything to stand in the way or to make you go back to the way things were before."

It was Mrs. Rodriguez, the widow in the apartment below theirs, who helped them. Her parents had come from the island, but she could speak little Spanish herself. The evening after the funeral she came to the door, took a deep breath, and said shyly, "They need someone else at the hotel and I thought of you and spoke to the boss and he said to bring you tomorrow. It isn't such bad work. You don't need any experience, they'll train you, and I just thought you might be wanting a job. There are others there who just speak Spanish. . . ."

When José had translated this offer for his mother, she burst into tears and a flood of Spanish gratitude.

Somehow the landlord had been persuaded to wait a few more weeks for the rent money. They had managed, and they could still walk with pride, for they had been through the hardest of times without getting into welfare. José and Tomás had done their best to teach Mami English as fast as they improved their own. No longer were they told to "leave *that* speech at the school" as they had been on the island.

But, thought José, listening to the wind pushing at the panes and forcing its way around the newspapers his mother had put over the windows, it was not enough. They ate, yet always they were hungry. They had clothes, but not many. José and Tomás had coats nearly down to their ankles so they could be worn

15

other winters. They didn't mind this, but José wondered if the coats could possibly last until they fit. His mother had a coat that had been warm enough in the spring but was not meant for December.

And they had a home. In some ways it was better than the shack they had lived in on the island. But there the outdoors was as much home as the inside. Here the rain still came down through the roof in summer, because they lived on the top floor. But that was the least of it. Beds could be moved away from the leaks. There was no way to escape the winter cold. It even came through the walls in the places where the plaster was gone. Home should be a place to be warm, José thought.

"It is up to me to get Mami a blanket," he said to himself. "Father would have done it if he had lived to see a winter in this cold place. Christmas is coming in six more days. God, let me get Mami a blanket for Christmas."

José fell asleep trying to think of ways to earn the money for a blanket. The next morning he thought about it as he folded the mattress and dragged it to a corner, out of the way.

José and Tomás started the dishes while their mother packed three lunches in paper bags.

"I will do that when I am through with the lunch making," she said. "It is no work for man or boy. You will have enough of that when you go to be soldiers."

"*Por favor*, no, Mami," said José. "It is good for

us to do this. See how clean my hands become. And Tomás, how good the exercise is for his arms."

Tomás rubbed at a dish so briskly he almost dropped it.

"So although I am the mother here, you two are the fathers, eh?" Mami said. "You tell me what I can and cannot do."

Tomás and José giggled.

"You should not push yourselves forward so with your elders," their mother said. "I must punish you." And she laughed as she lightly tapped the ear of José.

"Me too," Tomás said. "Punish me too!"

—"Yes, indeed I will," said Mami, and she kissed his forehead. "And now I must go. Be good at the school, you two, and come straight home."

"Yes, Mami," Tomás promised. José said nothing. An idea was beginning to come, and he was not sure he could safely promise to come straight home. His mother did not notice. She hurried out so she would not be late for work. It was very important that she be there at the right time. On the island it would not matter so much, but here it was important.

José thought of his plan as he walked with Tomás to the school, and while his teacher talked.

"José, you are not paying attention," said the teacher. "Tell me about Columbus."

"In 1493 he came to Puerto Rico," José said quickly.

The class laughed and even the teacher smiled.

"If you had been listening," Mrs. Adams said, "you would know that Columbus is the capital of Ohio."

"I am sorry," said José. But he went on thinking his own thoughts. He couldn't stop.

In the afternoon José thought about it while they

worked on the cardboard boxes they were making for
their mothers for Christmas. Today they did the paint-
ing. José painted his red and white for the hot sun
shining on a sandy beach. Tomorrow they would add
the varnish, and the boxes would be done.

"This is a fine present," José thought, "and so
is the calendar with the picture of flowers pasted on it
that Tomás is making. But Mami shall have an even
finer present—the finest she ever dreamed of."

By the time school was over José knew what he had to do. He had to find a job from someone in the neighborhood, and he had to be through working by six when Mami came home.

The biggest problem he could see was his brother. Tomás could not keep anything inside his head. Everything he knew came pouring out of his mouth. José did not like to have secrets from his mother, but if she knew what he wanted to do, she would say, "You are too little, *mi hombrecito*, to do so much worrying." And she would forbid him to get a job, and there would be no blanket.

As they left the school, José said, "Tomás, can you keep a secret?"

"Sure," Tomás said. "Anyway, who would I tell?"

"I mean a secret from Mami," his brother replied.

"Oh. But that is all right," Tomás said. "I have not told her of the box you are making, and I will not tell her."

"It is not the box," José said. "And you told her about what you are making. Who knows what you will tell next?"

"It is my present," said Tomás. "I can tell her about my own present. If you tell me the secret, I won't tell."

"Well, I will tell you part of it," José said. "And if you keep that part, I will tell you the rest tomorrow."

"Tell me all of it now," Tomás pleaded. "I won't tell."

"No. Here is the part for now," José said as they reached their building. "I am not coming up with you. I will be home when Mami comes. If you do not tell her, I will tell you the rest tomorrow. It is a good secret, one she will like if she does not know of it too soon."

Tomás stared at his brother. They were *niños de casa*, children of the home, and they were allowed to go nowhere but to the school without their mother. All kinds of evil could happen in the city, their mother said, and the only way to stay out of trouble was to stay away from it. This was not so hard in the winter when it was too cold to play outside, but it was agony in the summer and fall to look out the window and see the other children playing and hear their taunts. Often the brothers had argued with their mother about this, and even disobeyed a few times—but always together.

"I will go with you," Tomás said. "Whatever it is, I will help you."

"You can help by going up without asking questions now. I must hurry. Go on, now, I am bigger than you and I say it must be so." José took the string with the key on it from around his neck and gave it to his brother.

Tomás sulked, but he turned and went into the building without another word.

José started at the bakery, but they had no job
for him. The Chinese laundry had no job. The *bodega*
had no job. At the movie theater José said, "I can
sweep. I can do a lot of things." No, he was too little.

José asked everyone on the block— "No, *mu-
chacho*, no job."

On the corner was a man selling Christmas trees.

"Could I help?" José asked. "Do you have a job for me? I will do anything."

"I'm sorry, son," said the man. "Business is very bad. There are too many people selling Christmas trees, and not enough people with money to buy them.

"Oh," said José. "Well, thank you anyway." He turned away slowly. He had been so sure he could get a job somewhere.

"Wait a minute," said the man. "Tell you what. If you can find a way to sell these trees, I'll give you a dime for each one you get rid of."

José wanted to shout, to sing—he had a job! But he kept the shouting inside.

"I will sell them," he told the man.

José picked up a little tree and stood in the way of the people walking by. "Buy your Christmas tree now," he said. "Very special trees. Very cheap."

A few people smiled at him, but nobody stopped.

"See what I mean?" said the man. "Nobody wants to buy. I'm sorry, son."

26

José kept trying as long as he could. In a little while Mr. Sands told him it was a few minutes to six. José said, "Can I come back tomorrow afternoon?"

"Any time," Mr. Sands said. "If you have good luck, it will be my good luck, too."

José ran all the way home and up the stairs. His mother would be home any minute. He was glad to see that Tomás had set up the dominoes on the table as though two were playing. "That was a good thought," he said, as he sat down opposite his brother and picked up a domino. Now if only Tomás could keep the secret to himself.

That night Tomás did not tell the secret, and the more he did not tell it, the more he thought about it. He hardly dared look at his mother, and after dinner, as she sewed a button on his coat, she asked him what was wrong.

"You are sick," she said, "or you have done something bad. Which is it?"

Tomás looked pleadingly at José, but José could not help him.

"Come now," Mami said. "Come sit by me and tell me. There is nothing so bad you cannot tell me. Are you afraid I will punish you? But what of that? After the punishing, it is all over and we will never speak of it again. It will be like it never was. Now tell me."

Tomás sat next to his mother and stared at the needle going in and out. At last he said, "I am sorry the button came off."

"That is not it," said his mother. "Buttons go on and off. It is no matter. Now tell me."

Tomás looked away from his mother and said, "I wish I had not told you about the calendar. It is no longer a surprise."

His mother laughed. "Is that all? You are a silly *niño* to worry about that. I have already forgotten what you told me about it. And anyway, I have not seen the picture, and that is the important part. Now go play. It is nearly bedtime. Do not scare me so with such nonsense."

José breathed a sigh. It was all right so far.

The next day at school José figured out how many trees he would have to sell for a blanket.

"If I had five dollars," he told himself, "I should be able to buy a good warm blanket."

José had to multiply ten cents many times before he found that fifty of them would make five dollars. Fifty trees. And he had not sold one.

"José, what are you doing?" asked his teacher.

"Multiplying," said José.

"We finished arithmetic an hour ago," she said.

"I am sorry," he said. But he had his answer.

After school he met Tomás, and as they walked home he told his brother about the blanket.

"Someday," José continued, "Mami shall have a fine apartment, with an elevator instead of all those stairs to go up, and a warm coat, and a new tooth for the one in front that is gone. And I will take her back to the island. Someday I shall find a way."

—Tomás said angrily, "Yes, you will do these fine things for Mami, and what will be left for me to do? Why do I have to be too little always for everything?"

José stood in front of his brother. "Listen to me, Tomás," he said. "Did I say I could do all these things alone? Could I get the money for the blanket if you do not help me by keeping it a secret? The blanket will be from both of us. I shall tell Mami that it is so."

"I could help you sell trees. Or I could get a job of my own," said Tomás.

"No, it is better this way," José said. "Then one of us will be obeying Mami, and that is a good thing."

"All right," said Tomás. "But you do not have to take me home. I can go by myself."

"Yes, you know the way," José said. "And you are not so little any more. Today, to start with, you can walk by yourself ahead of me and I will follow. Then we shall see."

"O.K.," Tomás said. He went on ahead. But soon he stopped and waited for his brother. "I do not like to walk by myself," he said. "There is no one to talk to."

"Then we will walk together. After this no one will take anybody home. We will walk together as brothers should," José said.

José left his brother at the apartment and hurried to the Christmas tree stand. He took his little tree and stepped in front of everyone who went by.

"Very special trees. Very cheap," he called.

Some people scowled at him as he stood in their way. But by 5:45 he had sold two trees. One of them he had delivered and the lady had given him a quarter. Mr. Sands told him he could keep any money he made delivering trees.

"Can you hold the money for me for a while?" asked José. He didn't know where he could hide it at home.

"Sure," said Mr. Sands. "Just say the word when you want it."

José hurried home. Tomás opened the door before he could ring the bell.

"Forty-five cents," José shouted.

"That is good?" Tomás asked.

José sighed. "Not very. But it is a start." Forty-five cents, and three more days to go.

The next afternoon the first person he saw coming toward the Christmas tree stand was Mrs. Rodriguez. He tried to hide his face behind the tree he was holding, but it was too late.

"José, is that you? Does your mother know you are not at home? She didn't say anything to me about it," Mrs. Rodriguez said.

José peered out between the branches. "I have never seen you come home this early," he said. "I hope it does not mean you are ill."

Mrs. Rodriguez laughed. "Don't sidetrack the issue. As a matter of fact, I don't feel nearly as ill now as I did when I talked to the boss about it. I think I even feel well enough to get some Christmas shopping done. Now I've told you my guilty secret, you tell me yours. You know me well enough by now to know that I won't tell your mother if I don't have to."

There was no choice, so José told her about the blanket. "If you tell her," he said, "she will make me stop."

"Well, I'll tell you something, José. It's been a long time since I had a tree, living alone the way I do. But every Christmas day I wish I had one to cheer me up. Even though I'll be spending Christmas with you people, I guess it would be a good thing for me to have a tree this year. If I buy it from you, I won't dare tell your mother, having helped you."

José gladly sold her a tree and told her he would leave it by her door on his way home. After that he sold six little trees and the biggest tree in the stand. Mr. Sands gave him twenty cents for selling the big tree. He made fifteen cents delivering one tree and a quarter for another. But he would not take any money from Mrs. Rodriguez. His mother would be very angry if he did that.

A dollar and seventy-five cents, and two more days.

That evening the secret weighed heavily on Tomás. It was such a long time to keep a secret. It was not right for him to know something Mother could not be told. His guilt took away his appetite and his speech.

At the end of supper José and Tomás started to leave the table.

"No," said their mother, "you will stay where you are. Tomás, you will tell me what is the matter with you. For days you, and your brother as well, have been acting strange, and tonight strangest of all. What is it, Tomás?"

Tomás was silent, staring miserably at his plate.

His mother moved her chair to face him and put her strong worn hands on his shoulders. "See, here we are, just the two of us, and it is time for the truth to pass between us. Was it the truth you told me the other day when I asked you what was wrong?"

Tomás shook his head. "It was the truth, but not that truth," he whispered. All at once he buried his face in his mother's lap and howled, "Don't make me tell, please don't make me. There is a secret and it is not mine. I can't tell you any more."

Mami ran her fingers gently through his hair and looked at José.

There was silence for a while. Tomás sat up and also stared at his brother.

"Mami?" said José.

"Yes, my son."

"Mami, I am not the boss of this family. That is you. But I am the man of the family—maybe a little man, but still a man. There is no help for it. And because of this, there are things that I must do."

"But to have a secret from me, Jose? This you must do?"

"The secret is not a bad one. I think it is a good one. But I do not know what you would say. So I have made it a secret until it is over. It is not something I am doing for me, but for someone else."

"For me, Jose?"

"Yes, Mami. And if you say I must tell, I will. But I hope you will not say that."

His mother rubbed her forehead as if she could rub all the worry away. "Without a father in the family it is hard to know what to do. And living in a foreign country, everything is so strange and different than what one is used to—"

"But I have told you before. It is not a foreign country. It is ours, as much as the island. We are citizens, all of us," Jose said.

"Yes, we are citizens," his mother said angrily. "I come here a citizen and have to learn to speak all over again. And we must live by the clock as if we are machines. Remember, Jose, when the bus at the settlement house was to take you and Tomas to the zoo? You were just a little late, a half of an hour late, and the bus was gone without you. And your teacher tells me

I do not even know the name of my son, because she does not care how many names he has in the middle, he has to go by his last name—"

"But she said later she was sorry," Jose pointed out. "She put down the right name on the card." The teacher had been new and it was hard for her to understand that the last name was the name of the mother and the name in the middle that of the father. But after many Puerto Rican parents had argued with her about it, she had at last understood.

His mother went on as though he had not spoken. "And people do not like us. They say the only reason a *puertorriqueno* comes here is to get on the welfare and let the city take care of him. Your father dreamed for so many years of coming here where there are more schools, more places to work and live, and good hospitals when you are sick. All your father wanted was to work hard and make a good life for his sons. When he won that money, his dreams came true. We will stay because he would want it so. Anyway," she finished drearily, "there is no money to go home."

Jose and Tomas were silent. Their mother seldom acted like this. Jose knew his mother missed the island, but he had not known she felt this bad about it.

After a while Mami said lightly, "I am sorry—such a way to talk, and so soon before Christmas. I should be thinking of the good things, not the bad."

"You cannot help it if you feel that way," said José. "But I wish—"

"Yes, I know. You wish you could tell me how I am wrong. I wish that too. Maybe someday you will, but now for your secret. I know littler and littler every day, but one thing I know, my boys are good boys. If I did not know this— Well, anyway, you may have your secret. I trust you."

"You will not be sorry," José said.

He went to bed with a lighter heart than he had had for days, but still he did not know if he would be able to buy the blanket. Perhaps he could earn the money by Three Kings Day. That would give him until January 6th. But they had decided they would have gifts only on Christmas this year. There was not enough money to have gifts on both, and the church was having a party for children on Three Kings Day at which there would be presents. Anyway, no one would buy Christmas trees after Christmas.

The next day he sold four trees and made twenty cents for delivering one. Two dollars and thirty-five cents.

Mami made no mention of the secret. After they ate their rice and beans, they took out the box with the *nacimiento*, the Christmas scene, and carefully unwrapped each figure. On top of the dresser they arranged the figures of Mary, Joseph, the Infant, and the donkey. The Three Kings were put on the farthest windowsill. Each day they would be moved a little closer until it was time for them to arrive at the manger. When it had been arranged and rearranged to everyone's satisfaction, they stood back to admire their work.

38

It made Christmas seem very near. Already José could almost taste the roast pork. It would not be the same as a whole roast pig cooked outdoors. He wondered what the landlord would say if they had tried to raise a pig in their apartment. Still he was looking forward to the roast pork. And they would have *arroz con dulce*, which was something like a rice pudding with cinnamon in it.

But if he could, he would have pushed Christmas further away to give him more time to earn the money for the blanket.

José prayed very hard that night. "God, you must know that tomorrow is Christmas Eve and I am not even halfway to a blanket. A good warm blanket, God, not another cotton one. It is true I do not have to go to school tomorrow, but my mother will be home at one. Something has to happen before one. Amen."

José thought over his prayer and added, "*Por favor* —please!" Maybe two languages would help.

The next morning José and Tomás insisted on doing the dishes again and hurried their mother off to work. They finished quickly.

Before he left, José said, "I want you to pray hard, Tomás—as hard as you have ever prayed before. Only that way will a blanket come."

"I will," promised Tomás.

"Very good, Tomás, and now I go to the Christmas tree place."

Mr. Sands had four trees for him to deliver and that gave him eighty cents.

For two hours Jose stood in the cold and sold three trees. Not many people went by. And yet a few blocks away, there would be many people. Always there were many people on that street. Suddenly Jose felt like shouting again.

"May I take a tree down to 125th Street?" he asked Mr. Sands.

"Sure. Why not? Good luck," Mr. Sands said.

Jose hurried. As soon as he sold this tree, he would go back for another. Maybe he could still do it.

He reached 125th Street and walked down it a way to a very busy place. Standing in the middle of the sidewalk, he shouted, "Very special trees. Very cheap. Last day."

But everyone was hurrying, hurrying, hurrying. No one would stop. The people looked straight ahead

in sad or angry stares. That was the way they always looked walking down the street, but José did not know what they were angry about or why they never smiled.

He stood for an hour, stamping his feet to get warm. This was the coldest day he had ever known. He remembered, on the island, being told about the cold in New York, but he had not understood that it could be anything like this.

It began to snow, slowly at first, and then harder and harder. His feet and hands were prickly from the cold, and the flakes of snow stabbed at his cheeks.

It was twelve o'clock, he saw by a clock in a store window. José needed so badly to cry. He tried to keep it inside. He remembered what his mother always said, "When you feel like crying, sing—sing the tears away." Maybe that was why she sang so much to them at night—songs from the distant island.

José closed his eyes and began a song about the island, a sad song to be singing so far away. He sang of Puerto Rico as an image of the lost paradise, where flowers and fruits are always growing, and where the sun is born and shines and dies. This only made José all the colder.

"Not for anything would I change this land where I had the privilege to be born!" he sang in Spanish. But he was not there, he was here, and the song did not help the sadness to go away.

Very quietly he began a happy song they had learned at school:

"Oh, Christmas tree, oh, Christmas tree . . ." and then louder and louder as the tears tried more and more to come—

"HOW LOVELY ARE YOUR BRANCHES . . ."

As he finished, he felt the sting of tears on his cheeks and opened his eyes. There was a crowd around him and the tree. He looked at it. Its branches were covered with snow, adding a new beauty to it.

A woman asked him why he was standing there singing and holding a Christmas tree.

"Very special trees. Very cheap. Last day," José rattled off, his voice trembling with his shivering body.

"I'll take it!" five people said at once.

"Is this your last tree?" a man asked.

"Oh, no," said José. "Just a short way from here I have many fine trees. I will show you." And, still holding the tree, he started walking, praying they would follow. They did!

"You sing with me," José said shyly. The people laughed, grinned at each other, and all joined in:

"Oh, come, all you faithful . . ."

As they walked, other people stopped, stared, asked questions, followed, and joined in the singing, as if hypnotized.

"What's this, a parade?" asked a policeman. He scratched his head dubiously and followed.

They sang "We Three Kings" and "O Little Town of Bethlehem" before they reached the stand.

José sold many trees. "Tomás must be praying awfully hard," he thought.

"Merry Christmas, Merry Christmas!" everyone called as they left.

"What am I gonna do with this tree," the policeman muttered, dragging it away. "We already have one at home. Must be out of my mind."

José counted the money the man gave him. Four dollars and fifty-five cents. Not what he had wanted, but maybe close enough.

"Thank you very much," said José.

"Thank *you*," said the man. "You deserve a bonus. Pick out any tree you want. How about this one?" and he pulled out the biggest tree left.

José started to thank him again, but the man said, "You earned it, José. And now tell me. What did you need the money for so badly? I knew you were desperate that first day. I don't like to nose into someone else's business, but maybe I can help you. You've certainly helped me."

José told him about the blanket. "With this," he said, holding out the money in his hand, "I think maybe I can buy what I want."

"Hmm," said Mr. Sands. "That's not an awful lot. I could add a little to it."

José shook his head. "I have earned this," he said, "and I will see what it can buy."

"Well, that's a good way to be," Mr. Sands said. "But tell you why I said I might be able to help you. I've got a brother-in-law who owns a store on 125th. He knows about you and he was saying last night he wished his kids had half your gumption. I'll bet he would give you a discount on a blanket. Here, I'll give you a note for him." Mr. Sands wrote out a note on a scrap of paper and handed it to José, giving him directions on how to get to the store.

José hurried off, too excited to think of taking the tree home first. By the time he reached the store, his shoulders ached, but he hardly noticed.

He made his way slowly, apologizing frequently whenever he hit someone with the tree, to the curtain counter where Mr. Sands' brother-in-law stood. Mr. Andrews read the note and grinned.

"So you're José," he said, holding out his hand. "Glad to meet you. Let's get this tree of yours out of the way behind the counter before you knock down the store. C'mon, I'll take you to the blanket section."

48

"Color?" Mr. Andrews asked when they reached
the blankets.

"Red," José said quickly.

"Something very nice in red," Mr. Andrews said
to a saleswoman.

José had his blanket. He tried to thank Mr. Andrews.

"*Por nada*," Mr. Andrews said. "You see—I know
a little of your language. Anyhow, good luck and
Merry Christmas."

"Same to you," said José.

José went home dragging the tree in one arm and holding the blanket box in the other. He was out of breath when he reached the building where he lived. After resting a moment he called, "Tomás, Tomás, come down and help me."

It was Mami who came to the window. José had forgotten the time. "José! What have you done!" she screamed. She closed the window and in a moment she and Tomás were downstairs.

His mother took the tree and Tomás, the box with the blanket. On the way upstairs his mother gabbled in Spanish, "I get home and neither of you are here so I run out to the street and there is Tomás strolling home and I am about to hit him, although I never hit my boys in the street the way some mothers do, when he says he has been in the church praying so how can I hit him for that—and he will say nothing of where his brother is but what I want to know is, have you been stealing, José—I must have an answer for how otherwise could you get this tree and what is in the box—answer me that . . ."

As soon as they were in their room, José took the box from his brother, tore it open, and let the blanket spill out to the floor.

"*Madre de Dios!*" his mother said prayerfully.

José told her all that had happened, but it was not until the third time he repeated it that it reached his mother's ears.

She spread the blanket out on the bed and stroked

it. "Oh, *mi hombrecito*, what can I say?" she said, hugging him.

"It is nothing," said José. "The man of the family should provide such things as blankets without long speeches being made. And it is from Tomás, too—from both of us."

"And I was so worried it would be a sad Christmas. I was able to buy so little," said Mami. "But suddenly

all is happiness. Oh, your father would be so proud of his sons!''

They put the Christmas tree in a bucket of water and leaned it against a corner of the room.

"We should put things on it, things of all colors," Tomás said.

"No," said his mother. "It is beautiful the way it is. See how the whole room is brighter. And tonight we shall stand around it and sing all the songs *de Navidad* we know, and more besides," Mami said grandly, throwing out her arms.

"Tomorrow you can open the presents we made at school," said Tomás.

"Just possibly there will be something for the man of the family and his fine brother," Mami said.

That evening, in the middle of a song, she stopped ng. "I have just had a thought," she announced.

They waited for the thought to become words.

"Is it a good thing for the man of the family to be a *niño de casa*?" she asked.

José and Tomás laughed gleefully.

"Be serious now," said their mother. "I want you to promise me that you will always stay together when I am not here. Is it a promise?"

The brothers promised this.

"All right then," Mami said. "You are no longer *niños de casa*. When the days are warmer, you may play outside until I return from work."

54

That night José whispered to his mother, "Are you asleep?"

"I am too happy for that," she said.

"Is it such a cold land still?" he whispered.

"Are you telling your mother what to think now? You are indeed a bad boy."

"*Sí*, Mami."

"Well, then, go to sleep."

"*Buenas noches.*"

"*Buenas noches*, my son."

There was no shivering that night. It was as though they were lying on the white sands of the beach with the sun overhead.

LA TERRUCA

Poema de VIRGILIO DÁVILA
(1869-1943)

Música de BRAULIO DUEÑO COLÓN
(1854-1934)

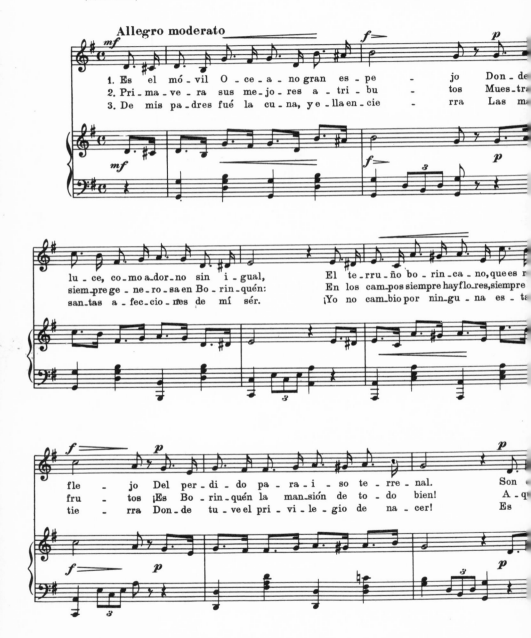

Allegro moderato

1. Es el mó - vil O - ce - a - no gran es - pe - jo Don de
2. Pri - ma - ve - ra sus me - jo - res a - tri - bu - tos Mues tra
3. De mis pa - dres fué la cu - na, y e - lla en cie - rra Las m

lu - ce, co - mo a - dor - no sin i - gual, El te - rru - ño bo - rin - ca - no, que es
siem - pre ge - ne - ro - sa en Bo - rin - quén: En los cam - pos siempre hay flo - res, siempre
san - tas a - fec - cio - nes de mí sér. ¡Yo no cam - bio por nin - gu - na es - ta

fle - jo Del per - di - do pa - ra - i - so te - rre - nal. Son
fru - tos ¡Es Bo - rin - quén la man - sión de to - do bien! A - q
tie - rra Don - de tu - ve el pri - vi - le - gio de na - cer! Es

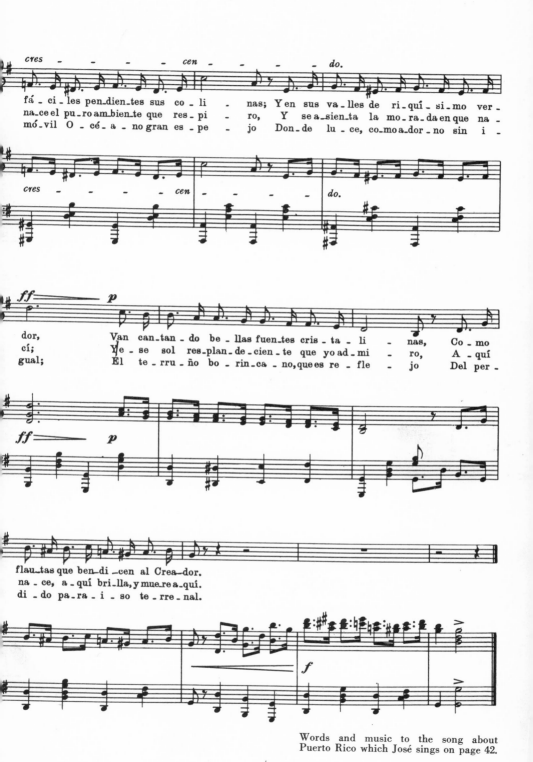

cres _ _ _ _ cen _ _ _ do.

fá _ ci _ les pen_dien_tes sus co _ li _ nas; Y en sus va _ lles de ri_quí _ si_mo ver_
na_ce el pu_ro am_bien_te que res_pi _ ro, Y se a_sien_ta la mo_ra_da en que na _
mó_vil O _ cé _ a _ no gran es_pe _ jo Don_de lu _ ce, co_mo a_dor _ no sin i _

cres _ _ _ _ cen _ _ _ do.

dor, Van can_tan _ do be _ llas fuen_tes cris _ ta _ li _ nas, Co _ mo
cí; Y e _ se sol res_plan_de_cien_te que yo ad _ mi _ ro, A _ quí
gual; El te _ rru _ ño bo _ rin_ca _ no, que es re _ fle _ jo Del per_

flau_tas que ben_di _ cen al Crea_dor.
na _ ce, a _ quí bri_lla, y mue_re a_quí.
di _ do pa_ra _ i _ so te _ rre _ nal.

Words and music to the song about
Puerto Rico which José sings on page 42.

Other books by Joan M. Lexau